THE COURAGEOUS CORGI

The "Tail" of a Little Dog with a Big Heart

Lea Herrick

The Courageous Corgi
By Lea Herrick

Copyright 2004
All rights reserved
Library of Congress Catalog Card Number 2004101978

ISBN   1-930052-17-0

Cherokee Books
231 Meadow Ridge Pkwy • Dover, DE 19904

Table of Contents

Acknowledgments/Dedications

"Bless the Beasts and the Children, For in this World, They have No Voice, They Have No Choice."

To my beloved corgis who saved me when I was lost and have since crossed over the "Rainbow Bridge."

To my dear parents who instilled in me my love of animals ...may I never turn my back on an animal or person in need.

To my loving husband, my brother and devoted friends, who daily help me overcome my illness and allow me to believe that anything is possible.

Special thanks to Nora Howell for the cover and her illustrations and to James Milton Hanna for giving me a chance and showing me the way.

Introduction

    The Courageous Corgi is based on a true story of two rescue Pembroke Welsh corgis from Wales. Although their early beginnings in Wales are unknown, from the time of their purchase by a sailor and their coming to America – to their rescue and finding a "forever home" – this is the account of the corgis' journey. Truth sometimes is sadder than fiction, but the author wished to write the story of these brave, little dogs as a tribute to the years of love and devotion that they shared with her.

It is a book for all ages that touches on issues that many wish to ignore or perhaps are just too painful to acknowledge. It is hoped that through this book and the work of animal rescue organizations, others may be saved from the pain and suffering that so many unwanted, abused and neglected animals endure each year.

LH
2004

Chapter One

Life in Wales

Once upon a time, on a windswept island in a far-away land called Wales, there lived a little corgi dog named Ramsey. Ramsey was the most beautiful reddish/brown color, with a crisp white streak from the top of his head to the tip of his nose and four white stubby paws that looked as though he had just splashed through a can of paint. Corgis, you know, don't have a real tail, only a tiny stump; so, when Ramsey was happy, he would wag his entire back end, running and jumping into the air like a small, gleeful dancing bear!

Ramsey was a relatively young pup, as dogs go, with only a year or two of dog wisdom behind him. He spent his days on a farm in the lush green rolling hills of the countryside, playing and frolicking with his farmer's sheep. Corgis were supposed to herd cattle by circling the cows and nipping at their heels, but Ramsey really preferred to bask in the warm sunshine, taking a sunbath in the green grass and sleepily gazing in the direction of those pesky sheep.

Ramsey really did like the sheep although he would never admit that to another corgi and occasionally, just to keep them on their toes, he would let out a loud playful bark, running and chasing them, watching the rams and ewes run together in one great large group. Then he would stop, being ever quite satisfied that those sheep wouldn't become too comfortable in one spot as long as he was the keeper of the fields. Ramsey even rationalized that he was doing a great service by keeping them in shape, preparing the sheep to run to safety should a real predator, like a wild dog or wolf, happen to wander into the field and spy them. Of course, he couldn't actually remember when this had happened, but it made him feel better about his playful antics.

It was truly a dog's life for Ramsey in Wales, and he envisioned that even Dog Heaven couldn't be better than this. His farmer was so good to him, saving him all the best scraps of meat from the dinnertable and occasionally even giving him fresh eggs from their hens and cheese made with milk from their goats.

On cold mornings, the farmer's wife would make a little extra hot porridge and take his favorite dish and place a large, heaping serving in it with a chunk of fresh churned butter on top. Ramsey would lap it all up and when he was just as full as a tick, he would lay on the soft colorful braided rug right next to the wood stove in the kitchen and smell the wonderful aromas of bread baking and pot roast slowly simmering on top of the stove, with the sweet scent of carrots and potatoes wafting through the air all day until it was ready for supper. It was so warm and cozy in the cottage and after eating such a hearty breakfast, it was all Ramsey could do to try and stay awake in the kitchen. As hard as he fought it, he usually drifted off into a lovely morning nap, catching a little doggy shut-eye and dreaming of what he was going to eat for supper and of warmer days, when he would be more inclined to go outside and play with the sheep again.

Life as it was, could have seemingly gone on forever like this for Ramsey, and so he thought it would, but destiny was about to intervene and change everything in Ramsey's world very soon!

Chapter Two

A Spring Blizzard

Spring was just around the corner but it was still much colder then Ramsey preferred. Ramsey loved crisp, cool weather as that was truly "corgi-weather," but this day, there was a nip in the air that was more biting than usual and the wind had begun to whip up, howling and blowing from the North in gusts and gales that were more reminiscent of the beginning of winter rather than the start of spring.

Ramsey was quite content to lay by the crackling fire of the wood stove where it was so toasty warm as he really didn't see the need to venture outside in this weather. He had already taken his morning nap and devoured a few crusts of homemade bread dunked in the creamy potato soup that the farmer's wife had prepared for lunch. It was a most enjoyable afternoon, but as the day passed, the weather was taking a turn for the worse, and the little cottage shook with the gale force winds and the panes of glass in the windows began to rattle so much so that Ramsey thought they would certainly break. He also began to hear a strange pinging noise with the sounds of ice crystals outside hitting the window glass. It wasn't long before snow began to fall and sure enough, it appeared as though they were in for an early spring blizzard.

The weather worsened and Ramsey could sense that something was wrong as the farmer's wife started to pace back and forth in the small cottage, looking out the icy windows for some sign of her husband, the old farmer. The afternoon wore on and as the snow deepened, the farmer's wife was almost beside herself, opening the little cottage door, calling out the farmer's name but to no avail. It was beginning to grow dark and Ramsey knew that even though the snow was deeper than he was, he had to venture outside and head toward the fields to find his master and get the sheep to safety.

Everytime the farmer's wife opened the cottage door looking for her spouse, she carefully guarded the entrance as she didn't want her cherished dog to run out in the storm, fearing that with his small size, Ramsey would surely get lost, buried in the deep drifting snow, never to be found again until the late spring thaw. She couldn't bear the thought of that on top of everything else, as she was sick with worry about her dear husband. He was usually inside by now, washing up and getting ready for supper. The farmer's wife tried to think of a logical reason, other than the obvious, as to why her man was so late, but try as she might, she couldn't think of anything except this terrible dread that something awful had happened to him.

Ramsey watched her ever so closely as she continued to pace in the cottage, wringing her furrowed hands, and at last when she went to the door and opened it slightly to look out into the blowing and drifting snow, Ramsey made his break and squeezed by her long woolen skirt, running as fast as his little legs could take him out into the bitter cold evening. His mistress cried out for Ramsey to come back into the warmth and safety of the cottage, but Ramsey ignored her pleas, heartbreaking as they were, because he knew it was his duty to find his master and their sheep.

Chapter Three

The Accident

The air was frigid and the snow was falling so heavily that it was almost blinding. The wind was coming off the sea and the little dog felt a shiver run through him, but he kept going, more determined than ever to find the old farmer. Darkness was settling in and Ramsey could hear the ocean waves crashing against the rocks on the shoreline over the hills, with no sign of the storm abating. The frozen ice crystals were clinging to his fur as they fell from the ever-darkening sky and Ramsey now had to expend a lot of his energy jumping and leaping through the heavy drifts of snow. His ears were so cold and the fur around his muzzle and eyes were crusting over with ice. Ramsey stopped short, perking his pointy little ears to the wind, listening to what he thought were the bleating sounds of sheep off in the distance. Yes, it was them! He never thought he would be so happy to hear those sheep!

Ramsey bounded through the deep snow, struggling to make it over the hill to the glen where the sheep must be. As he came over the crest, he saw them all snuggled together. With the snow so deep and the sheep the color of creamy buttermilk, they almost blended into the drifts, but Ramsey could still make out their wooly shapes in the fading twilight. He scampered down the steep hill weary from the effort that it took his small body to reach the lambs, but at

the same time he was overjoyed with relief. As he drew near
to the huddled mass, he suddenly realized that something
was terribly amiss. He barked and barked, running about
and gathering all the sheep together, ready for the long trek
back to the cottage and barn; but where was his master? He
should have been watching over the sheep, tending them.
Ramsey stood at attention, listening as the gales howled and
whistled past the flock, but still Ramsey heard no sound
from his master. He frantically circled the sheep and knew
that he was going to have to leave them to run over the next
hill to look for his master there.

He pressed on through the ever-deepening snow,
searching the fields as he headed back up the steep hill and
suddenly he thought he spied the shape of a person laying
face down immediately on the other side of the crest.
Ramsey was so exhausted that undoubtedly he must be see-

ing things. He raced down the knoll and there at the bottom lay his master, motionless and nearly covered with snow. Ramsey nudged his master's face over and over again, but his master never moved. He desperately began licking the old farmer's weathered face, hoping against hope that this might awaken him, but it did not. Ramsey tried everything that he could think of to help his master. He barked and yelped and when that didn't work, he grabbed his master's woolen jacket with his strong jaws and teeth and tried to drag him in the hopes that his friend would wake up from this horrid stillness as if this had all just been a bad dream.

It was growing darker and colder by the minute and the storm was raging, becoming more powerful with each passing gale. Ramsey was covered with snow, and his fur was becoming so encrusted with ice that it felt as though he was carrying the weight of the world on his back. Ramsey did not realize that in that instant, his life would dramatically change forever. Finally, Ramsey knew that he was turning so cold and his coat so laden with snow that his energy was waning. He had to do something quickly or they all would perish in the blackness of this terrible storm.

Chapter Four

The Arduous Journey Home

Ramsey's master had always taught him that the safety of the flock was the most important thing, so he made the decision to try to make it back over the knoll to get the sheep, herd them to the cottage to safety and get help for his beloved master. It was a daunting task but he bravely faced the fierce storm and headed into it. He ran as fast as his tired little body would carry him, but it was becoming more difficult for him to move as his legs and his paws were all but frozen in the deep snow, and they felt as though they had lead weights tied to them.

Ramsey trudged ahead barely able to make it over the knoll back to the sheep. He finally reached them and forced himself to gather them together, nipping at their heels, circling and barking commands to get them to budge to make the long arduous journey home. It was as though something came over Ramsey and he found the strength to keep his sheep moving through the deepening snowdrifts and wind.

A little lamb on its tiny wobbly legs could barely keep up with the flock, trying desperately to lie down in the snow, but Ramsey was like a little powerhouse, refusing to let it go down to its death. He barked at the little lamb and nudged it and eventually brought it back together with his mother and the rest of the fold. He continued to herd and drive the sheep and finally Ramsey managed to see the warm glow of a tiny lantern at his master's cottage in the distance. Determined to bring them all safely home and into their barn, Ramsey never lost sight of the tiny lantern, as it was his guiding light in the storm.

Ramsey could smell the wood smoke of the fireplace and knew that he and the flock were really home. The master's wife, who had been fraught with worry, had been watching out the tiny, icy window of her cottage, barely able to see from the blinding snow drifting against the thatched walls of the dwelling. At last, she saw the little dog and the sheep coming over the hills and flung open the cottage door, wrapping herself up in a long woolen shawl, running to the barnyard to open up the fence gate for the animals to come inside the pen and into the warmth and security of the huge old wooden barn.

The sheep took refuge inside the shelter from the howling wind and lay on piles of straw, exhausted from such a difficult journey home. Ramsey wanted to do the same, but one glance at his master's wife's face said it all. She spoke in an almost crying tone, asking Ramsey where his master was. Ramsey knew he had to go back out in the perilous snowstorm and lead her to him at once, praying that maybe she could rouse the old farmer and bring him home out of harm's way before it was too late.

Chapter Five

Life Changed One Night

Ramsey began to bark frantically and headed back toward the barn door to be let out into the tempest storm, hoping that the farmer's wife would understand and get help and follow him. Somehow she knew what Ramsey was trying to tell her. The telephone lines had been down for hours so there was no use even wasting any more time trying to reach someone that way.

She jumped in an old pickup truck that the farmer used to go to town in for his necessary errands, found the keys under the driver's seat, grabbed Ramsey and headed into the night toward a neighbor's house across the vale. Ramsey was growing increasing weary and at the same time very nervous, knowing that they were in a race against time if there was any chance of saving his beloved master. The farmer's wife gave the old truck everything she had, steering it over the hills and through drifts of snow on the way to the neighbor's cottage. It seemed as though it was taking forever and Ramsey waited impatiently while the farmer's wife hurried out of the truck and down a snow covered path to the neighbor's door.

No sooner had she left the truck and in an instant, a gruff, elderly man jumped in the driver's seat, and the farmer's wife flew into the passenger's side, looking desperately into Ramsey's eyes, pleading with him to lead the way in the wintry gale.

Ramsey knew that the only way to show them was for him to leap out of the truck and into the cold dark storm, running through the night, with the truck following behind him. Ramsey didn't know if he had the strength to do this again, but realized he had to muster every ounce of courage in his body and do this one last thing for his beloved master. The truck followed swiftly behind the little dog in the darkness, shining its headlights on the path ahead that Ramsey was forging through the snow. Over hills and dales, into valleys he ran and finally Ramsey recognized the knoll where his master lay. He began barking furiously, hoping that the neighbor and the farmer's wife would see what he saw and understand that they needed to get out of the truck and follow him to a spot that was now so snow covered that the figure lying on the ground was all but invisible.

Both the neighbor and the farmer's wife left the truck and followed the dog to the place where he was circling in a crazy fashion, howling and baying as if the world was coming to an end. Ramsey again tried to stir his friend by licking the poor old farmer's face, which by now was a bluish color and cold as ice. The neighbor hollered for him to get away, and threw the little dog across the snow. In a fit of anger, Ramsey raced back over to his master, and by now his mistress was kneeling down on the ground, cradling her husband's face and head, wailing in the most mournful way he had ever heard, calling the old farmer's name over and over again. The neighbor lifted his master's lifeless body out of the snow and placed him in the pickup truck, covering him with blankets that were in the back. The farmer's wife climbed back in the truck and before Ramsey knew what had happened, they drove off into the darkness, leaving the small dog behind in the freezing night. Then the truck stopped abruptly, and his master's wife flung open her door, calling for Ramsey to get into the truck, which he did, before it sped away into the blinding snowstorm.

Chapter Six

If Tears Could Turn Back Time

The farmer's wife picked up Ramsey and held him on her lap, sobbing ever so softly as the truck grinded and sputtered its way over the snowy hills toward home. Ramsey didn't really understand what was happening and why everyone was so sad. And he especially didn't understand why his master had not awakened from his sleep and was covered up completely in blankets, with not even his weathered old face or cap showing.

Ramsey lay quietly on the farmer's wife's rumpled woolen skirt, nestled in her arms, listening to her sobs.

Ramsey was so exhausted and confused and he just wanted to lie down next to a warm fire and sleep for hours, thinking that when he awoke, this would all be just a bad dream. But that didn't happen.

They hastened toward the cottage, and when they finally arrived back home, Ramsey jumped out of the truck as they stopped outside the front door and watched while the two of them carried the body of his master into the house and laid him on a wooden cot by the fireplace.

Chapter Seven

Loss and Confusion

From then on, everything seemed a blur to the poor little dog. People began to come and go from the cottage, and the old country doctor arrived with his black leather bag, but eerily, the doctor never needed anything from the bag and placed the blanket back over his poor master's face. Ramsey sensed that something was horribly wrong and everyone that came to the door left weeping and trying to comfort his master's wife, who had barely spoken a word the rest of the night.

The next day, when the storm subsided, things became even grimmer. A gentleman dressed all in black drove up in an old wood paneled station wagon, and he lifted his beloved master onto a stretcher and took him away, never to return again to the cottage and farm that he had loved so well.

This was all too much for a little dog to comprehend and Ramsey sat quietly by the hearth, whimpering, never lifting his head from the floor or taking his eyes off the farmer's wife. What was going on? Why was everyone so sad? Hadn't he done a good thing by leading them to his master? And when was his master going to come through the door, with his woolen jacket and cap, carrying his walking stick, and taking his boots off by the fire, warming his toes under Ramsey's furry little body?

Something had changed and Ramsey waited pensively, looking for some sign that things would eventually go back to the way they were before that dreadful snowstorm on that long, desolate night in Wales.

Chapter Eight

The Funeral

Things did not get better over the course of the next few days or weeks. In fact, Ramsey was so confused that he really did not know what to make of this anymore. There was a flurry of activity and everyone coming to visit the poor farmer's wife was dressed in black and spoke in soft whispers at the cottage.

Ramsey followed a procession of people up a hill overlooking the ocean and the fields where sheep had grazed and his master had tended them and where Ramsey had gleefully frolicked in the sunshine as a pup, and it was the most beautiful spot for miles around. In this procession, four of the village men carried a heavy wooden casket on their shoulders and they lowered the box into the ground and covered it with sod. People knelt quietly on the land and the parish priest said prayers aloud, which were difficult to hear through the muffled sobs of the farmer's wife and friends. Truly this couldn't be where his master was, but Ramsey remembered that this was the same spot where he had gone that night in the snowstorm to find him. The farmer's wife placed one small white flower on the mound of earth and this must have been the first blossom that had peeked up through the snow this spring, showing its newly formed petals to all who laid their eyes on it. It was such a thing of beauty and new life, and what irony that it should now lay on a mound of cold, dark earth. What a stark contrast it was on this chilly spring day. The farmer's wife turned and left, gazing back ever so slowly as she followed the rest of the procession back down the hill. The ocean spray from the rocks landed on Ramsey's fur, still bringing a chill to him this early spring day. Ramsey walked slowly beside his mistress and she occasionally glanced at him, reaching down to pat his head from time to time, amidst wiping soft tears from her eyes with a linen handkerchief. The village people left one by one and soon it was just Ramsey and his mistress alone in the tiny cottage.

Days passed and the farmer's wife barely ate anything, although she cooked all of Ramsey's favorite things to keep his strength up. The farmer's wife grew weaker and weaker and began to cough most of the night, soon becoming too frail to even lift her thin body out of bed. The neighbors came and insisted that she go into town to the hospital where the doctor could tend to her, as she simply was no longer able to care for herself, Ramsey or the flock of sheep. The day that she left, the gruff old neighbor across the vale came over to the cottage and brought a sailor with him who looked at Ramsey, pulling his cheeks and lips up, checking his teeth as if he was some horse! What on earth was happening now to him?

The neighbor and the sailor talked at great length and bartered back and forth until finally the sailor pulled out a handful of gold and silver coins, giving them to the neighbor. With that, the sailor bent down and picked Ramsey up, startling him, and headed toward the door. Where was this strange man dressed in this funny outfit taking him? Why was he leaving the cottage with him and where was his mistress? Shouldn't she be back soon to feed him his evening meal? The sailor placed Ramsey in his car in the back seat and Ramsey jumped up to look out the window and took what was to be his last glance at the tiny cottage and his sheep as they drove off down the dirt road, and evening began to fall.

Chapter Nine

Long Voyage Home

Ramsey never imagined that his life in Wales was over and that he would be crossing the ocean on a huge ship to begin life anew in a distant land. The Atlantic Ocean in early springtime can be very ominous and stormy, and Ramsey was placed in a cage on the deck of a large naval vessel to weather the long journey to his new home with the sailor who had purchased him from the gruff old neighbor in Wales.

Ramsey did not have a mean bone in his body, but sometimes dogs can just sense when they don't particularly care for someone, as everyone knows that not only is a dog man's best friend, but dogs are excellent judges of character too. The farmer's wife used to say, if there were more dogs in the world and fewer people, the world would be better off, and Ramsey was beginning to understand the meaning of that.

He was cold and wet from the ocean spray of the squalls and the waves crashing over the bow of the ship. He could barely move in this wire cage and what food the sailor brought to him made him sick with the rocking motion of the ship going from side to side. Ramsey thought he would surely die and maybe that might be a blessing under the circumstances. This was certainly not Wales and he missed both his beloved master and the farmer's wife so much, and even all those pesky sheep that used to give him fits when he attempted to herd them back to the barn, were looking pretty good to him right about now. The sheep really were fun to play with and pester and Ramsey daydreamed about his days back in Wales and envisioned that he was running in the fields, with the grass tickling his nose and toes, and the sweet blossoms would be giving off their glorious scent by now like perfume, wafting heavily through the spring-time air.

Oh how he missed his farm in Wales and wished that he could turn back the hands of time, to the way things used to be – just he and his master tending the flock on the lush green hills of Wales. Oh, when was this journey going to end? Little did Ramsey know that it was only just beginning.

Chapter Ten

Statue in the Mist

It seemed as though days passed and Ramsey was so cold, wet and seasick that he barely realized one morning at dawn, as the fog was just beginning to lift over the Atlantic, that the ship started to slow its speed. Sailors came running up on deck and all seemed to turn in the same direction as if they were trying to catch a glimpse of something. Surely, there was nothing to see in the midst of this large ocean, as Ramsey could tell you first hand, other than an occasional passing school of dolphins or porpoises swimming and jumping in the air doing their acrobatics until they swam off.

He listened intently, with his ears straining to hear conversation to give him some clue as to what all the sighing was about. Then, through the wires of his tiny cage, Ramsey suddenly saw a clearing and a great white figure in the distance on the horizon, looking as if it were coming right out of the sea...a figure larger than life! Certainly, this was the biggest creature he had ever seen and Ramsey became very afraid at first, not understanding what this creature was.

The sailors on deck seemed absolutely joyous and began celebrating with cheers, laughter, and some even wiping away tears from their eyes. He heard others singing, "Give me your tired, your poor, your huddled masses yearning to breathe free...send me the homeless, tempest, tossed to me, I lift my lamp beside the golden door."

Ramsey really didn't understand the meaning of any of this and finally he heard a sailor say that he was never so glad to see "Lady Liberty" as he was now after months away from his home in America. Could Ramsey have heard this correctly? Were they really coming into America? He had heard his master and others from the village talk about this distant land and its vast opportunities for anyone who dared make the voyage here, but he just couldn't believe that this is where the ship was docking.

Indeed, they were docking, and as the fog lifted, he saw the twinkling lights of a city in the distance, looking like a million little points of light, like the stars on a starry night. They passed a huge, ominous looking brick building in the harbor that appeared very scary to Ramsey, and he heard the sailors telling tales of the immigrants coming through Ellis Island before entry into this new land. He hoped that he would not have to go there as it frightened him just to look at this, like some large looming castle or fortress in the harbor. He didn't think that anything good could possibly come from going to a place like that.

Ramsey couldn't take it all in fast enough. Everything seemed so expansive compared to the tiny cottage in Wales. It appeared as though they were now speeding into the port and he heard the sailors talking about docking in Brooklyn. What a strange name that was. Everything seemed to be very intimidating for the small little dog and he wondered what lie ahead for him in this new land. One thing for sure, undeniably it was going to be an adventure!

Chapter Eleven

Sailors Galore

Sailors were running busily around the vessel, throwing anchor down and tossing lines to those who were waiting at the dock, and the men were madly dashing about, gathering up their gear and duffel bags to depart the ship.

It seemed as though time stood still as Ramsey waited anxiously in his tiny crate, hoping that he would not be forgotten and left on the vessel. Finally, the sailor that brought him from Wales came and opened the small cage. Ramsey could barely straighten his tiny, chunky legs, and as he started to leap down, they went out from under him. It looked as though he was drunk and the sailor laughed, helping Ramsey to his feet, stating that he did not have his land legs yet, whatever that was. Ramsey was so wobbly and weak from the nine-day voyage that he could not believe that he was going to be on dry land again. He scurried down the gangplank next to the sailor, as he was now getting the knack of walking once more.

Ramsey could hardly believe all the sights and sounds of the bustling port and he did not know that this many people even existed in the world! Daylight was dawning and he did not understand why everyone was still not back in their cottages, fast asleep. The sailor called Ramsey to keep up with him, but Ramsey was low to the ground and there was so much activity with the longshoremen that he could barely see the bellbottomed pants legs of the sailor's uniform to follow.

Everyone was dressed in white with white caps so they really all looked alike, but Ramsey kept up, weaving in and out of the crowd, desperately trying to keep pace with the sailor. Ramsey just could not think of him as his new master, as he missed his old farmer back in Wales so much, knowing that no one could ever take his place in Ramsey's heart. But, he might as well get on with it and stop thinking about what was never to be again. Instead, he began to get excited about all the smells, sights and sounds in this strange new land. Ramsey was also beginning to get his appetite back and as they passed a huge open-air fish market, the sailor stopped and bought some fresh bread and cheese and shared this with the little dog. Maybe this sailor wasn't going to be all bad. Ramsey would have to reserve judgment on that for now.

This sailor seemed very self-assured and was walking apart from the rest of the sailors as if he were headed in a different direction than the others. Ramsey continued to follow him after their small respite, wondering where they were going, but as long as it was not back on that ship, he didn't care. He was so very far from home; he still could not believe that he was in America! Wait until the farmer's wife heard about this! Why, she would be in awe as he had watched the expression on her face as she sat for hours by the fire listening to the neighbor ladies and their tales of relatives who had come to this new land. No one would really believe that he was here.

He needed to focus on these new surroundings as lurking in the shadows of the docks, there were gangs of men who looked very frightening and scary, huddled together in small groups, whispering in hushed tones. The sailor decided to pick Ramsey up and carry him under his arm when one unkempt man appeared out of a dark corner of an alley and lunged toward the sailor and the small dog. The man in the shadows really looked very unsavory and you could smell the pungent odor of alcohol on him. The man stumbled and the sailor yelled something at him, and the man swore at them, but then he staggered back into the shadows. Ramsey would be happy to leave this area and soon!

Finally, the sailor hailed a strange looking vehicle with a man driving and hopped in with Ramsey still under his arm. The sailor asked the driver to take them to the train station, and Ramsey hoped that conditions for him would be more pleasing on a train than they were on the ship. It was still not completely light outside and Ramsey curled up on the sailor's lap to keep warm on this damp, misty morning and before long fell fast asleep. It was so good to be off that ship and Ramsey felt that even though the ride was long and bumpy over the cobblestone streets, he was ever so glad to be able to shut his eyes and dream again about days passed and of days to come. He was rudely awakened from this wonderful nap by the screeching of brakes as the cab came to an abrupt halt, and as the sailor paid the driver the fare, he grabbed Ramsey and his duffel bag and leapt out of the car.

There they were at the train station, and Ramsey had never seen so much activity, except of course at the dock. Many men and women in uniform were waiting at the depot and Ramsey couldn't keep up with all the different colors of uniforms, nor all the people there, many speaking languages that he had never heard before. What a sight for a little dog! Suddenly Ramsey heard a loud whistle and the chugging of the train coming down the tracks. People were scurrying everywhere and in one fell swoop, the sailor snatched Ramsey up and placed him inside the large duffel bag, pulling it almost closed, with only Ramsey's snout sticking up through the opening of the bag. The sailor admonished Ramsey to be very quiet and not make even a peep, or they would both be thrown off the train and have a very, very long walk to Norfolk, Virginia.

What another strange name for a place, and Ramsey couldn't imagine what that place must be like. He obeyed the sailor, lying quietly in the bag, and when the train doors opened, there was never such a crunch of people in uniform, going in all directions, trying to come aboard the train.

The conductor was taking tickets from those who were not in uniform and the sailor placed the duffel bag with Ramsey inside of it at his feet, while the sailor stood holding onto a ceiling strap to steady himself. The ride seemed endless and there was much merriment inside the train car, with men and women laughing gaily and talking about their experiences abroad. What a great group of people, Ramsey thought, as they were certainly very different from the farmers and shepherds in the quaint little villages in Wales. Everyone here seemed so young and vibrant, full of energy and anticipation of the new day. Ramsey wished that he could see out of the bag, and out the train windows, but he knew he had to be still or else! He longed to see everything about this land, and he wondered if it was young, like all the people on the train. Maybe this wasn't going to be so bad after all.

Ramsey was up for anything at this point and was beginning to feel some hunger pangs again, as that bread and cheese didn't go very far to fill up a corgi belly! He dozed on and off to the rhythm of the train and it lulled him into the sweetest corgi dreams he had had in many months.

He awoke and could feel the sunlight streaming into the train windows, warming his furry little body through the duffel bag. Someone came through the car selling food and his sailor bought two ham and cheese sandwiches and some cookies and proceeded to bend down ever so slowly stuffing one of the sandwiches and a cookie inside the duffel for Ramsey. Ramsey hadn't really tasted anything like this in

Wales, but he was hungry and devoured every last morsel of his snack, licking his chops to ensure that nary a crumb was left behind on his muzzle.

The sailor reached down and petted Ramsey on the top of his head and Ramsey was beginning to warm up to him, wagging his little stump of a tail inside the bag. He was starting to get his strength back and wanted oh so badly to jump out of the bag and prance happily throughout the train car, dancing up on his hind legs like he had done so many times in the fields of Wales, but he knew he didn't dare! He really was starting to have a marvelous time and the antici-pation of finally reaching his new destination was almost too much for a little corgi to bear. Ramsey let out the small-est of woofs, but quickly remembered himself as the sailor glared down at him.

It seemed like an eternity and finally Ramsey could feel the train slowing down to a stop. The sailor picked up the duffel bag and when the doors opened, he swung down the steps onto the platform just as the train began to pull away from the station and out of sight. Was this Norfolk?

Ramsey was let out of the bag, and once again he saw sailors everywhere. He sure hoped that this didn't mean that he was going back on a ship and his mind raced as to his next plan of action if that be the case. He decided that he absolutely would not go back in a cage for another long voyage, although the thought of going back to Wales still loomed in his mind. That really didn't make any sense to him, so he quickly dispelled that notion and tried not to think of any unpleasantries on this new day. Things were going to be better, he just knew it.

The sailor made his way out of the station and onto the street, where they walked for what seemed forever. They came to a small bungalow on a narrow little alleyway and the sailor reached into his pocket, taking out a set of keys. They walked up the steps of the house, the sailor opened the door and Ramsey followed him obediently inside as if he belonged there too. The sailor then threw his gear down in the tiny living room and slumped over on the sofa, stretching out the length of it and promptly fell asleep, snoring loud enough to wake the dead.

Ramsey already had his doggy nap on the train and he was very eager to explore his new surroundings. He didn't have time to waste sleeping just yet until he investigated every nook and cranny of the bungalow, memorizing every item in his path throughout the house. It was a nice place, but the furnishings were somewhat stark and it lacked the coziness of the cottage in Wales, but it would have to do for now.

Hours passed and Ramsey amused himself while the sailor slept, walking around and around the bungalow, searching for a stray crumb or errant critter to occupy himself with until the sailor awoke. He loved to explore new places, so the hours passed quite hastily for this little corgi. He watched a lone insect crawl across the floor and played with it a while before pouncing on it like a duck on a June bug. This was great fun for him and the day had passed quickly with the shadows of twilight now coming through the windows.

His sailor finally stirred and sat up on the couch. He motioned for Ramsey to stay at the house, and he went out the front door, returning in a short time with two big juicy steaks for dinner. Ramsey and the sailor feasted all evening on steak, potatoes and carrots and although he was used to mutton, he really didn't find the steak to be at all offensive!

Nightfall had settled in and the street lamps in the alleyway were now lit. As he curled up next to the sofa for the night, Ramsey went back over the day's events in his mind, hardly believing that so much had happened in such a short span of time, as he went round and around in a circle, scooching the scatter rug in just the right position for bedtime as he drifted off to sleep.

Chapter Twelve

A New Home

Several months went by and Ramsey was beginning to bond with his new master, playing in the small backyard every morning before the sailor went to work, and every evening when he returned home. They had settled into a regular routine and although it was not Wales and he still missed his former master and mistress, Ramsey really did not have any complaints about Norfolk. Sometimes, the weather even reminded him a little bit of Wales when the fog and mist rolled in from the ocean in the evening and stayed until the morning's light.

Ramsey slept during the day, eagerly awaiting dinnertime when the sailor returned from work with their supper each night. It was a pleasant life, although an uneventful one, until one day when there was a knock on the door and his master received new orders. The sailor appeared both pleased and sad at the same time and Ramsey did not know what to make of this. He heard the man talk of an island out in the ocean called Bermuda and from what his expression conveyed, it must be a lovely place to visit. But the sailor looked very apprehensive and as he stared down at Ramsey, he had the most concerned look upon his face that he had ever witnessed from this rather happy go' lucky man.

The sailor was so perplexed that night that his sleep

was very restless and Ramsey sensed that something was terribly wrong. His new master had orders to ship out the next morning and when he awoke, the sailor was madly rushing around the small house, gathering his uniforms and gear together. But what would happen to this small little dog? Would he be orphaned again?

The sailor flew out the back door and ran across the alleyway to the neighbor's bungalow. It seemed like an eternity before he returned, but the little corgi did not know what was in store for him. Upon command, Ramsey timidly followed the sailor across the alley and over to the neighbor's yard, where he suddenly spied a large pen surrounded by chicken wire in the backyard with a gate that latched. The sailor told Ramsey that he must go inside the pen and he was so very sorry, but Ramsey was not allowed to go to Bermuda with him. The sailor mentioned something about a quarantine, which Ramsey did not understand at all. The neighbor would tend to him until his master returned from the sea.

Ramsey balked and immediately tried to flee, attempting to turn and run before the gate could close behind him, but it was too late and the sailor grabbed Ramsey by the nape of the neck and pushed his little rump inside the pen and slammed the gate shut. Ramsey had no idea what was happening, but one thing he did know – he did not like this at all! This was certainly a terrible state of affairs and he felt trapped like the wolves that his old farmer in Wales would sometimes catch in order to protect their flock of sheep. Ramsey wasn't a wolf...he had never injured another animal ever, and he did not understand what he had done to deserve this treatment. Who would look after him now that autumn was settling in and the days and nights were growing longer and colder? He was a wonderful com-

44

panion and had done everything that this new master had asked of him. Why, oh why, was he now relegated to the cold, dark dampness of the outdoors? Didn't these people understand that his place was inside, guarding his master as he had always done back in Wales and here in America?

The sailor took one last longing look at Ramsey in the pen and wiped a tear from his eyes before he turned and walked with trepidation back across the alley and out of sight. Ramsey stood at the gate whimpering ever so softly as his heart was breaking. Sadness was not new to this little corgi, nor had he any idea what the days ahead would now bring. He only knew that misfortune had once again befallen him.

Chapter Thirteen

A Sad Retreat

The autumn days and nights stretched into the depths of winter and poor little Ramsey dog laid in that same pen every day and every night through all types of weather. The wind howled and the rain poured and the neighbor was rarely home.

Many days, Ramsey begged for a fresh bowl of water to drink or some leftover table scraps to eat, as he had never been so hungry or thirsty in his entire life. There was no shelter to speak of and Ramsey dug a hole in the dirt and crouched his body low into the ground to stay warm and away from the gales of winter. It was a terrible life for a little dog and his tiny bones began to ache and ache and some days his back was so stiff that he could barely straighten it to stretch.

To make matters worse, stray animals would torment Ramsey while he was in the pen and there was little he could do to protect himself. Someone in the neighborhood had a large black dog that was allowed to roam free, terrorizing anyone who crossed paths with it. Sadly, that dog also suffered from neglect and abuse as it was just as mean and ornery an animal as you'd ever see, which is really not a dog's true nature. Dogs are normally very social creatures and just love to be loved. One day, this black dog charged viciously toward poor Ramsey's pen at a full run, snarling and gnashing his teeth through the wire in an attempt to get at Ramsey. Ramsey bravely defended his area and hoped that this interloper would not break through the pen. Finally, the black dog gave up and moved on, but oh, what a frightening experience this was for the little corgi!

Another time, a big gray and white striped cat climbed over the wire and into Ramsey's pen in the far corner. What a surprise both animals had when they met eye-to-eye in the center! Ramsey could not imagine what possessed this cat to climb into his territory, but then again, one never knows why cats do anything that they do as they are fiercely independent and have minds that only they can figure out.

Needless to say, there was a large scuffle, with fur flying in every direction, barking and hissing, and claws scratching until finally the battered cat ran back up the wire and over and out the top of the pen in a gallop that would make a race horse envious. Ramsey later saw that cat with six baby kittens trailing behind her in the distance and figured that she must have been hungry too, looking desperately for some food and water so that both she and her babies wouldn't starve. Regrettably, there are too many animals that come into the world with no one to look after them or love them, and Ramsey understood all too well what that was like as he lived each day subjected to the unrelenting elements with no one to comfort and care for him.

Winter turned to spring, and still no sign of his master but at least the weather had broken some. Without a doghouse, the spring rains drenched Ramsey and he shivered and remained wet and cold most of the time. His fur was matted with mud and debris and no amount of Ramsey's licking could groom his coat back to the beautiful red and white color that it had once been. As summer came, there were actually days when Ramsey wished that winter was back, as without shade or a dog house in his pen, the sun blazed down violently on his little body with flies biting him, and it was all Ramsey could do to stay alive from the blistering heat. There were times when he threw himself into the dirty water dish just to try and cool down and Ramsey began to drift off, imagining that he was back in Wales with his beloved master and mistress, chasing the sheep over the hills and dales. Then he would come back to consciousness trembling and realize that he was still on earth but wondered why there was not a merciful God who would relieve him of his misery here. He whined and whimpered until he didn't have the strength anymore to even get up to his feet to eat.

Then something phenomenal happened and he thought that surely he must be dreaming or maybe he had entered through the Gates of the Kingdom and he was finally in Doggy Heaven. A lady came in a vehicle and after arguing with the neighbor and showing him a paper that stated the sailor gave her permission to take the little corgi, the neighbor reluctantly allowed her to scoop Ramsey up and whisk him away with her in her automobile. Ramsey's eyes were so cloudy and he was so weak and thin that his body hung limp as the kind lady picked him up and placed him on a blanket in the back seat of her automobile. It all seemed surreal and Ramsey had no choice but to lie there and hope that he was going to a better life.

Chapter Fourteen

Rescued at Last

A better life it was, or so Ramsey hoped it would be. At least he was finally free of that terrible pen and the raging heat and excruciating cold. As they rode in the automobile, Ramsey learned that they were going to a place called Baltimore and he listened with all the strength a little dog could muster even though he was too weak to lift his head. The lady that rescued him spoke to Ramsey in the most soothing melodic tones that he had ever heard. She reassured Ramsey that everything was going to be all right now and that they were heading to a lovely home in the countryside where he could recuperate from the terrible ordeal he had suffered this past year.

The lovely lady told Ramsey that he must hang on and not give up and she sped up the roadway heading north as dusk settled in. She talked and talked to the little dog lying on the seat and told Ramsey that they were taking him to a veterinarian to get him much needed medicine for his weak and tattered body, and that the kind doctor would soon make him feel so much better.

It seemed as though time stood still as Ramsey continued to fade in and out of consciousness on the automobile seat and nightfall began to approach. Ramsey had no idea how long they had been riding when he awoke and found himself on a table in a small office being examined by a kind elderly gentleman wearing a white smock with a stethoscope dangling from his neck. This must be the veterinarian that the lady had spoken about and the doctor was shaking his head in disbelief, listening to Ramsey's heart and lungs, unable to fathom how the little dog was even still alive! How could anyone have abandoned a beautiful corgi and left him out in a pen to suffer in all kinds of weather! For that matter, the veterinarian just kept repeating that he did not understand how anyone could do this to any animal! Ramsey was sure that the sailor that brought him to Norfolk from Wales had meant him no harm and never dreamed that he would be travelling to a place where he could not take him. How was the sailor to know that his neighbor would pretend that Ramsey was barely there in that horrible pen?

The doctor immediately began to treat Ramsey and gave him fluids to help bring the little dog back to life. Ramsey drifted off to sleep and the last thing he remembered hearing was the nice lady telling him that she would be back for him in a few days and that he should rest with the good doctor.

The veterinarian was far more worried than he let on to this lady and when he closed up the office for the night, he gently picked up Ramsey and wrapped him in a blanket and placed him in his truck with him, taking the ailing animal to his own home for the evening. The vet just did not feel comfortable leaving the helpless dog alone in a cage at the office all night by himself, and he would rest easier knowing that Ramsey was with him should he be needed to help the little corgi through this crisis that night.

Ramsey had a very restless night with fitful sleep, and the doctor put Ramsey on the mattress of his bed right next to him, with his arm resting ever so reassuringly on Ramsey's side, petting him throughout the night and checking his breathing and his heart with his stethoscope every hour to make sure that the brave dog had not left this world for the next. Knowing that this dear elderly vet cared so much for him, placing small sips of water on Ramsey's parched tongue, seemed to soothe Ramsey, and every so often he would gently lick the doctor's fingers.

As daylight began to appear through the crisp white curtains, the doctor checked Ramsey once more before he left the bedroom to get ready to return to his office for the new day's work. Ramsey actually lifted his head, and his eyes followed the vet as he went into the next room to make breakfast and ready himself for work.

The vet came back into the bedroom and seemed to be pleased that Ramsey was more alert than he had been the night before, and he brought with him a bowl of warm oatmeal to see whether the corgi was up to eating anything yet. Surprisingly, Ramsey smelled the aroma of the cereal and it seemed to trigger fond memories of porridge on the farm in Wales when the farmer's wife would place a big dollop of fresh butter on top of the cereal and give it to the little dog.

Why, with that, Ramsey lifted his head again, this time holding it up longer than he had been able to do earlier and stuck his snout right into the oatmeal, gingerly licking a small portion of it. This really wasn't at all bad, although it lacked that wonderful butter that he had so enjoyed in Wales, but it would do, for now. Ramsey could not eat it all, but the more he ate, the easier it became for him to do so. The kind doctor wrapped Ramsey up in the blanket again, and loaded him into his truck, taking him merrily to work at the animal hospital.

When the veterinarian arrived at his little office, he took Ramsey inside and made the nicest bed for him with quilts and blankets and placed the little dog right in the middle of it, like a giant nest and covered Ramsey with a small afghan to ensure that he didn't get a chill. Autumn was arriving and the air was beginning to get brisk and Ramsey remembered that this was "corgi-weather," the kind of days when it warmed by the afternoons, but was clear and crisp in the mornings and evenings, and the leaves turned their many shades of colors, looking ever so brilliant against the blue sky. Just thinking about that perked the little corgi up and maybe he was going to have a better life after all, just like he had in Wales.

This ritual of staying with the vet at work during the daytime, curling up in his nest bed watching all the comings and goings at the office, and heading home with this kind gentleman in the evenings, cuddling up next to him on his mattress at bedtime, went on for several weeks as Ramsey grew stronger and stronger, regaining so much of what his little body had lost in that pen in Norfolk.

All the people in the town knew their routine now, as Ramsey rode up in the front seat of the truck next to the doctor, looking out the window, sitting ever so prominently as if he were a person riding next to the vet rather than a dog. The townspeople would wave as they went to and from work, and Ramsey was enjoying himself immensely. It really was a sight to behold!

Ramsey was growing stronger with each passing day and he was now lapping up his food like there was no tomorrow. The vet hated to do this, and had been putting it off far too long already. One morning at the office, he made the call to the lady who had rescued Ramsey and told her that the dog was finally ready to leave his care, and that she could pick him up that evening. Ramsey could hardly believe what he was hearing as he just assumed that he would be here with this dear man forever as he genuinely adored him.

That evening, the lady came to the office and the vet tenderly stroked and petted Ramsey, touching the corgi's head with his lips as he leaned over and gently gave the little dog a kiss goodbye. The vet was wiping tears from his eyes with his handkerchief and pronounced to the lady that

Ramsey was now strong enough for her to find him his "forever home." The lady thanked the veterinarian over and over again and as she picked Ramsey up, Ramsey craned his head and neck around, desperately trying to get one last glimpse of the elderly vet who had saved his life.

Ramsey whined and woofed as he was placed in the lady's automobile and the vet turned slowly, closing the office door, never looking back. Little did Ramsey know that the doctor couldn't bear to watch her take Ramsey down the road as he was sobbing like he had never sobbed before. The dear veterinarian had so desperately wanted to keep Ramsey, but knew that Ramsey was just one of many kindred souls who would find their way to him, each one needing his constant, undivided attention and love, just as Ramsey had, to nurse them back to health. Ramsey needed a permanent home where he would be the center of that person's universe, where they could devote all their energies to making Ramsey happy, not having to share their time between so many sick and injured animals. The vet knew it was for the best, but still he cried like a baby. That Ramsey was one special dog, but aren't they all!

Chapter Fifteen

A Foster Home

Ramsey did not have too far to travel this time as he and the kind lady drove just a few miles down the road and pulled into a long driveway where a lovely old brick home stood by itself out in the country among the rolling green hills of northern Baltimore County. Ramsey stood up in the vehicle to get a better look out the window of the automobile before the lady placed a leash on Ramsey's collar. She opened the car door and Ramsey jumped down pensively, not knowing what to make of this. Ramsey had never had a leash on before so this was all new to him and he really did not think he liked this idea at all. But for now, he really had no choice and as he leapt out of the car, he decided that he was going to plant his feet firmly on the ground, lock his four little legs in a very straight and rigid position, and not move one inch. The lady gave a gentle tug on the leash and coaxed Ramsey to come up the walk with her to the door of this large and beautiful home. Finally, Ramsey relented and decided that there was nothing to be gained by being stubborn, although it just sometimes felt good to do so to a corgi.

Another lady, probably in her middle years, opened the front door and greeted them both with hugs, motioning them to follow her into her home. Ramsey gingerly accepted the invitation because it was growing dark and cold outside and he feared being left alone in a pen again like he had been in Norfolk. Once inside, Ramsey heard the yipping and yapping of at least ten or twelve other corgis and he saw little ones and big ones scurrying around and playing madly, frolicking and pulling on each other's tails and fur in one happy mob scene. They barely even noticed that Ramsey was there, although some of the larger and older male corgis immediately began to tense up and sniff the air around him. There were a few low guttural growls and snaps but the owner of this mob quickly admonished them to cease and desist and behave themselves or there would be no treats before bedtime tonight!

Well, that certainly seemed to do the trick and they all snapped to attention and each one sat down on their little haunches, wagging their stump of their tails, lining up, barely being able to contain themselves, wiggling around waiting for their mistress to stop her scolding so that they could once again begin running and playing in her large kitchen. What fun it appeared to be for all concerned, but Ramsey quickly reminded himself that he really did not want to be here and wasn't going to appear at all friendly, because maybe then, they would take him back to his dear friend, the elderly vet. Ramsey certainly didn't have time for all these puppies and their shenanigans as he had matured into quite a man and found that foolishness was for the very young.

The lady who rescued Ramsey from Norfolk recounted their tale to the mother of these young rascal corgis over a cup of hot tea and biscuits, and Ramsey was given a separate bowl of food and water, away from the other kids, on the sun porch which was delightfully decorated with wicker furniture and plants. While the two women and Ramsey ate out on the glassed-in porch, Ramsey finally decided to lie down and keep a watchful eye on the goings on while the ladies conversed and sipped their tea. The owner of all the corgis kept saying how sorry she was that Ramsey had to go through such a terrible ordeal, and she paused on numerous occasions to take a handkerchief from the sleeve of her sweater and wipe her moistened eyes as she looked down at Ramsey, while the other described their odyssey. Finally, the woman from the rescue organization bid them goodbye and reached down to pat Ramsey's fur, assuring him that this new lady was going to be his foster mother until that "forever home" was located that the vet had promised him. With that, the she fondly relinquished his care to his foster mom and turned and left, blowing Ramsey the sweetest kiss as she walked away.

Well, this couldn't be good, to be left with all the noise and racket of this corgi gang and Ramsey was feeling annoyed but rather comforted at the same time. Ramsey really had his nose quite out of joint, being left with the "wild bunch," but it was hard to stay mad as there was so much merriment in the house and you could sense the love of this woman for her canine friends, so Ramsey decided to accept the situation, especially since he was powerless to change it at this time.

It had grown quite late and the lady opened the back door, turning the flood light on and herded the throng of corgis outside in the huge fenced yard once more before bedtime. She took Ramsey out on his leash as he was totally unfamiliar with these new surroundings and she did not want him to get lost in the acreage.

With their duty done, there was a mad dash of corgis back into the house and into the kitchen for one last treat before lights out. Ramsey was going to sleep on a pile of warm soft blankets in a basket in his foster mother's bedroom. All this excitement had really tuckered Ramsey out and with that, he fell fast asleep for the rest of the night until he heard the barking and playful antics of the pups the following morning.

Chapter Sixteen

A Sudden Surprise

This new home was full of riotous behavior by the corgi pups and Ramsey soon fell into the groove as he was being observed and retrained with the rest of the pack. Ramsey learned how to walk and heel nicely on a leash and basic voice commands, and although he initially was not too fond of this regiment, he actually began to like it as it provided him with a sense of structure and security that he had not had in many, many months. Ramsey especially enjoyed the tiny treats that he and the pups received when they learned their lessons and the little corgi was determined that he was going to be the absolute best at the obedience training, and sure enough, he was!

Ramsey played like there was no tomorrow with the group of dogs and other than a few tussles to see who would be the first out the back door, there really was never any serious arguments among them, although at times when the play became rough, it sounded like a pack of wolves with all their bravado.

The rolling hills in the back acreage really did remind him somewhat of Wales and Ramsey occasionally found himself reminiscing about his days as a young lad with the farmer and their sheep. But he soon was jolted back to reality as one of the corgi pups would playfully grab his ear or take a flying leap and catapult over him in a gigantic somersault, with both of them rolling down the hill in one big ball of fur. It really was a sight to behold, but one by one, the pups were finding their permanent homes as winter was beginning to set in. Ramsey wondered if it would ever be his turn to go, but he really didn't mind staying here as long as there was at least one or two of the pups left to play with. He passed the time endlessly with mindless gymnastics and continued his obedience training. Surprises were going to be the order of the month and what happened next was almost unbelievable!

The lady of the house received a phone call and when she hung up the telephone, she went into the bedroom to find the paperwork that she had tucked into a drawer in the nightstand by her bed. She unfolded a document and read it thoroughly, shaking her head in disbelief but had a wonderfully wry smile and excited expression on her face.

Shortly thereafter, the doorbell rang and the lady from the rescue society that had brought Ramsey here came into the house carrying a smaller bundle of fur and mini version of Ramsey, except female, with four white paws and a silly little, funny face that was half white and half reddish tan that only a mother, or Ramsey, could love. The lady announced that this was "Skomer" and that she was also from Wales! Could it be? Could this possibly be Ramsey's long lost sister and littermate from Wales? She had been such a small little dog and the runt of the litter and when the farmer had bought Ramsey as a pup to herd his sheep, Skomer had been the last puppy left with the mother dog after all the others had gone to their respective farms with their new owners. Ramsey had been so sad to leave Skomer, worrying that with her small size, no one would want to buy her, as she was almost too little to tend a large flock by herself. He had never seen Skomer again after that day and now good fortune had brought brother and sister back together again in America, over a thousand miles from where they began their life in Wales.

When the rescue lady put Skomer down, Ramsey immediately ran to her and startled poor little Skomer as she stood frozen, shaking and trembling uncontrollably, being ever so frightened. Then suddenly Ramsey gave a big woof and instantly, Skomer recognized that bark as her brother's and they both began wagging their little stumps of their tails and licking each other over and over again, hardly believing this marvelous hand that fate had dealt them!

The two corgis jumped in glee and ran around and around circling each other and you never saw a happier reconciliation than the two of them giving each other a million doggy kisses. Both ladies wept and compared the papers they each had on the dogs. It was truly a miracle! What were the odds of these two dogs finding their way across the ocean and back to each other after all this time? Apparently, Skomer had also been owned by a sailor who could not keep her but she had suffered abuse from the next owner as you could tell by the way she cowered and shook whenever a leg or foot moved toward her that someone had been terribly cruel to her. Skomer would run and hide under a hutch or behind a chair with the slightest of noises so Ramsey knew that she had also had a very bad life, that is up until now.

Then one day, Ramsey sensed that something was going to be different. The lady of the house was obviously expecting company as she put all the remaining pups up and then spent her morning bathing and grooming Ramsey, placing a beautiful blue collar with a bright red bow on him and boy, he certainly looked like a million bucks. Then she did the same for Skomer, except hers was a beautiful red collar with a bright blue bow. She was as cute as a button! Ramsey had never been so handsome, nor Skomer so beautiful and corgis have this very distinct delicious doggy smell when they are oh so squeaky clean. Ramsey especially loved being towel dried and playfully grabbed one end of the towel, attempting to play tug-of-war with his foster mom, and having this bath just made him feel like a new man. He loved being so nice and fluffy looking and he waited in anticipation to see what the day was going to bring to them both. Ramsey could just sense that this was going to be their day!

Finally the doorbell rang and Ramsey could hear voices, but he and Skomer were kept in another room until the company had settled in. Then their foster mother came into the bedroom and called Ramsey and Skomer to follow her out to the glassed-in sun porch but they could not contain themselves any longer. Ramsey bolted past her and ran just as fast as his little corgi legs could take him to the porch and there sat not one, not two, but three people who all had their gazes fixed on this bundle of energy and fur. He scurried right up to the three of them seated on the couch, and with his hind legs stretching just as far as they could, he reached with his fore legs onto the sofa, straining his neck and muzzle up to the company as they bent down to pet him and slobbered them all with as many doggie kisses as he could muster in one fell swoop.

They giggled and laughed uproariously as they all snuggled down on the floor with Ramsey, petting him and talking to him in the sweetest tones. Skomer was much more shy and she gingerly came to the couch, but when she saw Ramsey madly kissing these people, she decided that it must be all right, so she joined in as well. This went on for what seemed an eternity and as the month was December and the days were long, shadows were beginning to fall and the father of the three stated that they best be taking their dogs and going home now. Ramsey stood there frozen, not understanding what the gentleman had meant. If they had dogs, why had they come to look at Ramsey and Skomer?

Then all of a sudden, as their foster mother put a leash on Ramsey and one on Skomer and handed them to the girl, Ramsey understood. Why, he was their dog now! Ramsey yipped for joy as he could just sense that these were good people...all three of them – the mother, father and daughter, and he could not wait to go home with them!

Their foster mom gave Ramsey and Skomer a hug good bye and bade them farewell as they all climbed into the automobile and headed out the drive on their way to Ramsey and Skomers' new home.

The ride seemed so very long and Ramsey and Skomer were as nervous as a cat in the back of the station wagon, not wanting to stand but not really wanting to sit either. Ramsey wanted to take this all in, watching these three folk and studying their every move and at the same time looking out the long side windows of the auto, watching the miles tick past as they headed down the road.

The girl, or perhaps, young woman, was more accurate, was sitting in the back seat closest to Ramsey and Skomer, petting their heads and talking to them all the way as if they were humans travelling with them. She would smile so nicely at Ramsey and the mother would turn every so often from the front seat to make sure that all was well with these new additions to the family. The father would sneak a glance at Ramsey and Skomer in his rear view mirror and seemed pleased that everyone was faring so well on the long journey home.

It was now very dark outside and Ramsey was still too excited to lay down and sleep but he was beginning to grow weary and hoped that they did not have too far to go. They crossed a huge body of water on the biggest bridge that Ramsey had ever seen and drove onto a peninsula through the countryside.

Finally they pulled down a gravel lane across from an old churchyard into a driveway and parked in front of a tiny yellow cottage with lace curtains and a porch lantern brightly burning to light the way up the walk. The three people got out of the car, with the father coming around the back of the automobile, opening the rear door of the station wagon and scooping Ramsey and Skomer up into his arms, carrying them up the walkway and into the little house.

The girl quickly turned on a lamp and closed the front door and the father placed the little dogs on the soft carpet, with the mother going into the kitchen to bring out a bowl of water for the dogs to quench their thirst after the long ride home.

The mother told Ramsey that both she and the daughter had lost their faithful corgis to old age in the past year and that the family had been so very sad and grieving until now, when they had chosen Ramsey and Skomer to be their special friends.

It had grown very late after the trek home and it was well past a corgi's bedtime. The mother and father bade the daughter, Ramsey and Skomer goodnight and turned and left the little house, heading out the drive and down the lane, with the sound of the auto now fading into the night.

Both the daughter and the corgis were so tired that they could barely make it down the hallway to the bedroom and as the daughter went to get into bed, she looked down at Ramsey and Skomer and made the instantaneous decision to pick them both up and place them on the bed with her, and Ramsey feeling right at home, decided to waddle right up to the pillow and curl up with his new mistress while Skomer scurried to the foot of the bed and all of them fell fast asleep. Ramsey and Skomer had found their "forever home" at last!

Chapter Seventeen

The "Forever Home"

Ramsey and Skomer grew to love their new mistress and their favorite part of every day was going outside in the lovely fenced yard in the woods, investigating every inch of the property, starting at one end of the fence with their noses pressed to the ground and walking the entire perimeter of the yard. They took such delight in ascertaining whether any little vermin or varmints, like those squirrel babies, were encroaching on their territory, and when they felt secure in the fact that all was well in their little area, they both would bound up the back stairs onto the porch and sit facing the yard, surveying every detail to ensure that nothing out of the way occurred on their watch.

Ramsey and Skomer were especially fond of all the birds that their mistress fed with the many bird feeders hanging from the trees, and the bright plumage of the birds' feathers was truly a sight to behold! There were chickadees, nuthatches, doves, wrens, mockingbirds, thrashers, catbirds, juncos, sparrows, cardinals, jays, goldfinches, flickers, and red-bellied and downy woodpeckers. The catbirds liked to play with the dogs, making the sound of a cat meowing, which easily excited Ramsey and Skomer, who ran around looking for that dreaded cat, but never finding one. Oh, what a trick that crazy catbird loved to play on those corgis! Every bird imaginable came to visit the feeders and in the wintertime, it was so crowded that the corgis laid on their cozy beds inside the house by the large sliding glass door, watching for hours and hours at the feast, with their feathered friends hopping all over the ground, making the cutest little three-toed tracks in the snow while others waited their turn at the feeders, lined up on the tree branches ever so patiently.

In the springtime, a stray hummingbird or two would come right up to the glass sliding door and sip very voraciously on the nectar that their mistress provided, ensuring that all the little birds had sustenance and food for their long migratory journeys home. Spring was also the time for the "turtle walks" as turtles plodded through the yard, making their way toward the creek for their yearly excursion to meet other turtles there. Ramsey and Skomer would bark and bark when they saw their turtle friends passing through and would get as close as they possibly could to the turtles, touching them with their noses. Unfortunately, there were times when the corgis got a little too close and they would accidentally flip a turtle upside down on its back. Then their mistress would have to go and right side the turtle and help it on its way to the other side of the fence. This prompted their mistress' favorite saying each night as she tucked Ramsey and Skomer into bed saying, "nite, nite, sleep tight – don't let the turtle bugs bite!" The corgis would then slobber her with kisses, wagging their little stumps with glee, before dozing off with oh so sweet doggy dreams. And on occasion, they were all lulled to sleep by the hooting of an owl in a tree close to the house.

Ramsey and Skomer could amuse themselves forever watching the comings and goings on their property and in the summertime, a swallowtail butterfly or two was even known to gently light on the backs of the corgis to rest a spell in between their busy flittering from butterfly bush to butterfly bush looking for nectar.

Autumn was also a special time for the corgis as the leaves of every red and golden hue looked like a collage of color and nothing pleased Ramsey and Skomer more than running and jumping into a huge pile of crisp and crinkly leaves.

Even though the yard was small, it was a delightful respite for all of God's little creatures and what nature had to offer. And the corgis loved to go outside when their mistress filled all the bird feeders and brought fresh water for the birds and the butterflies, but she had to be oh so careful, as when she was not watching, the corgis were gobbling up the seed she spread on the ground for the ground-feeding birds and mourning doves, faster than the birds could eat it! She would laughingly scold the corgis telling them that they were going to sprout wings and fly if they weren't careful! She would pretend to be mad at them as she laughed and giggled at their funny corgi ways, but she could not stay upset for more than a minute or two. She reveled in the fun and joy that her wonderful rescue canine friends brought to her and she could not imagine life without them now.

Ramsey and Skomer were always together and never left one another's side and their love for each other grew stronger and stronger with each passing day. What a stroke of good fortune that the two of them were reunited, living and flourishing in their "forever home" with their "forever mom"!

Sometimes they did get into trouble though when they became too rambunctious and played tug of war with each other and with anything they could get their little corgi teeth on. Then they would have to have a "time out" until they calmed down and composed themselves, but that never lasted very long.

It was a joyful home and the mistress and Ramsey and Skomer had such love and companionship that there was no place the three of them would rather be than in their little cottage in the woods, with their new-found Grammy and Grampy coming to visit them every day, bringing them all sorts of toys and homemade treats and biscuits to tickle their fancies and fill their bellies. Their mistress delighted in dressing up the dogs with ribbons and bows for every holiday and occasion, and they truly became part of the family, receiving presents for each of the special days of the calendar year and ice cream and cake, with birthday hats and a real birthday party on the anniversary of the little corgis' birth. What a wonderful life!

Chapter Eighteen

Tales of Joy

Corgis, of course, are known for their corgi-antics and Ramsey and Skomer became so secure and happy in their new "forever home" that being the mischievous little dogs that they were, they were subject to get into a few little "situations" from time to time. One evening, their mistress let the corgis out in the back yard to have their final romp before bedtime. It was winter and she had been sprinkling cracked corn on the ground for the bunnies to eat. Their mistress closed the sliding glass door and went back into the house, as it was too cold to wait outside while the little dogs played. She settled into the living room and started reading a book and as time passed, it dawned on her that things seemed a little too quiet for comfort out back. She went to the door and lo and behold, there was Skomer on the top step, looking into the slider holding a rabbit in her mouth!

The mistress was aghast and shrieked, telling Skomer to drop it immediately, which she did. However, when the rabbit hit the ground, it had only been stunned and came to its senses, making a mad dash for cover. Well, both corgis forgot themselves and took off after the rabbit, who became confused and raced in one direction, then another, trying to figure out how to get out of the fence. This only served to confound the corgis even more as they circled back and forth as in days of old, herding the little bunny first in one side of the yard, then the other. The more the bunny ran, the faster the corgis chased and all the running and circling back and forth was making them dizzy, with the corgis' tongues now hanging out, panting to try and catch their breath. It looked like a merry-go-round gone crazy! Finally, the little rabbit found an opening and ducked under the fence and out into the woods to safety. Both dogs literally dropped in their tracks panting and their mistress had to go out and retrieve them, scolding and laughing so hard that her sides hurt.

Another time, the little corgis and their mistress went down to visit and spend the night with their Grammy and Grampy. Oh, what a great time they were having and when all the house was quiet and their family fast asleep, the little corgis decided that they were all slept out for the evening and the dogs went down the stairs looking for something to get into. Their Grammy had a wonderful old oak rocking chair that she loved to sit and rock her corgi granddogs in. Ramsey and Skomer remembered this chair and decided it would be great fun to see it rock back and forth as they really loved that rocking motion. Skomer went to one end of the rocker and took one of the runners in her mouth, while Ramsey went to the other end of the runner, placing it in his mouth also. The two of them took turns pushing the runner up then down with their noses and mouths, with a back-and-forth motion, like a see saw. The chair started rocking to and fro, up and down, and the harder the corgis played, the faster the chair rocked. They had no way of slowing it down or stopping it except with their teeth. Soon they grew tired of this game and went off to amuse themselves with something else. The next morning when their Grammy awakened, she went down stairs as usual to get her cup of coffee and the first thing she saw was her lovely old rocking chair that was missing half its runner! She stooped down to examine it more closely and saw dozens of doggy teeth marks on what was left of the runner. Their Grampy came down the stairs and when he learned what had happened, he never laughed so hard! His only remark was, "At least the corgis had their roughage for the day!"

It was that time of year when Ramsey and Skomer had to go to the local veterinarian for their annual check-ups and booster shots. Ramsey and Skomer were very busy little dogs, you know, and really didn't have time to waste sitting in a vet's office. There were many things to do and so little time to do them. Well, the vet was behind schedule as he had tended to several emergencies earlier in the day, but the corgis didn't know that and were growing very impatient in the lobby of his office. Ramsey finally decided that he had been waiting so long that the little lobby was starting to become his domain and he staked himself next to the foyer by the door, guarding that area as if it were his own. Well, that wouldn't have been too much of a problem, except as more people brought their animals in for their appointments, who should they see immediately upon entry but Ramsey, stretched out at the entrance to the lobby, like a sentry guarding a gate. Ramsey had gained just a few pounds and his winter coat made him look like a big fluffy bear and a bit scary too. One by one, big dogs and little dogs would come in, take one look at Ramsey and stop dead in their tracks, refusing to go in any further or walk by him. The foyer was becoming crowded with dogs and a ruckus broke out. The vet and his assistant couldn't imagine what all the commotion was out there and came running, only to find Ramsey sitting like King Tut, guarding the keys to the kingdom while dogs of every sort and size were backing up trying to get out the door, shaking. They all laughed and Ramsey's mistress gathered Ramsey up, admonishing him about his naughty behaviour, with the veterinarian from then on, insisting that Ramsey come back to his office via another entrance away from the rest of the animals! That was certainly one way to keep the vet on schedule!

Sundays were a day of worship and the mistress and her parents usually went to church out in the countryside. This Sunday was no exception and after church, the three of them dined in a small café in town having a bite of lunch. Upon their return home, their mistress invited her parents to come in and see the corgis. As she opened her front door, her eyes gazed around the room in disbelief and she reeled back in a state of shock! At first she thought that a robber had broken into the house and ransacked it. Or maybe, some sort of a tornado had ripped through the dwelling while they were at church, destroying her every possession. Funny thing, the corgis were no where to be found. Things were too quiet and as she went over to the sofa to sit down, there came Ramsey and Skomer tumbling down the hall, holding the remnants of a stuffed rag doll called "Mr. Pumpkinhead" (because his head was a big stuffed orange pumpkin) in their mouths, still playing tug-of-war with him. Pieces of Mr. Pumpkinhead were strewn everywhere and his little blue overalls were drenched in doggy saliva. That was not all they had played tug-of-war with. Every magazine, book, basket, blanket, pillow, dog bed, trashcan, paper, curtain, afghan, and even the wicker bookshelf was demolished. It truly looked as if a bomb had gone off in the house with shreds of paper, cloth, stuffing and wicker everywhere! The little corgis had had great fun and couldn't understand why everyone would not appreciate this delightful game! Needless to say, after their mistress composed herself, (and she wasn't sure whether she should laugh or cry), she took what remained of Mr. Pumpkinhead out of the corgis' mouths and put an end to the tug-of-war games with a very big "time out" for Ramsey and Skomer in the kitchen behind a child gate. They looked so sad staring out from behind that gate as she cleaned up the disaster area, of what had once been her tidy little cottage. Their mistress couldn't stay angry with them for long as corgis are known for being quite gregarious and full of life! The house needed redecorating anyway, so you might just say that the corgis speeded up the process!

Many people place signs on their doors that say "No Soliciting." Well, one salesman found out the hard way when he decided to knock on the door to sell his wares. Being a persistent salesman, as so many are, when there was no answer at the front door, he decided to go around to the back door to try again. What the salesman didn't know was that corgis are generally opposed to anyone selling anything other than perhaps dog biscuits or doggy treats and toys. The salesman boldly opened up the gate to the back yard and stepped in, heading toward the back porch. What he didn't see were two corgis whose naps he had so rudely interrupted! Corgis love their corgi naps and disturbing them during this time was a woeful mistake on his part. Just as they saw him, the salesman spotted them. Corgis can sense fear in an individual and both dogs sprang to their feet, and as they did so, the salesman turned tail and ran toward the fence. Unfortunately, he was not quick enough and the corgis were right there. He tried to catapult over the fence, and almost cleared it unscathed, but his baggy trousers got caught on the top of the fence post and the little corgis gleefully jumped up and grabbed the seat of his pants, tearing a large hole the size of a softball in them. The salesman vaulted the rest of the way over the fence, minus a big piece of his pants, with the white of his underwear showing. He ran to his car so fast that he dropped his samples on the ground and tore out of the driveway, never to be seen or heard from again. Perhaps the sign should have read, "Beware of Corgis" rather than "No Solicitors"!

Happy "tales" and happy "wags" make for truly great corgi lives!

Chapter Nineteen

Cycles of Life

Life goes in cycles and you have to take the good with the bad sometimes, or so it seems. Ramsey and Skomer did not realize at the time, that they were brought to their little mistress for a reason and it was all part of God's plan.

One day, upon their mistress' return from work, she suddenly took ill and ended up in the hospital. For weeks, no one could figure out what was wrong with her and although Ramsey and Skomer wanted for naught while their Grammy and Grampy took care of them, they were at a loss to explain as to why their beloved mistress had grown so sick and pale. She was finally released from the hospital and had to be taken to her parents' home with her faithful companions, as she was too weak to care for herself or Ramsey and Skomer.

She developed respiratory problems that worsened over time, reacting to so many things that it became safer for her to stay in her parents home rather than venture out to have attack after attack, never knowing when her breathing difficulties would strike or how severe they would be. After her many visits to the emergency room at the local hospital, Ramsey and Skomer watched as their mistress became more frail and despondent. No one could seem to understand what had caused these terrible spells and it was becoming increasingly more difficult for their mistress to even find the strength to get out of bed in the morning and get dressed, with exhaustion overtaking her for most of the day. Only her parents, a couple of very close friends, and her beloved corgis understood the suffering that their mistress was experiencing.

Many days, all the little corgis could do to comfort her was to jump up on the sofa where she lay and lick her face ever so gently, letting her know that they understood and that they felt very sad too.

Finally, there was a break in the mystery when a young new doctor in the area found what was causing their mistress' illness. There had been a horrible industrial accident at her workplace where she was exposed to chemicals that caused her to develop a lung disease and many other health complications as a result of that calamity. The people at work knew what caused her sickness, but none came forward to speak the truth, letting everyone continue to believe that she must be suffering from some sort of mental infirmity. It was a very sad time in their mistress' and her adoring corgis lives, but with the help of good doctors, and the love and support of her parents, friends and faithful canine companions, she was finally able to return to work after many months of convalescence.

Unfortunately, their mistress' torment did not end there. Upon her return to work, she continued to experience breathing difficulties as no one still came forward to clean up the building after the accident. The workers there laughingly and jokingly called her the "girl in the bubble" because she reacted to almost everything, and it seemed like she needed to stay in a cocoon to prevent herself from being exposed to more chemicals which caused further decline in her health. People mocked her behind her back and made fun of her, finding great amusement in her predicament and disability. Many days, it was all she could do to make it home from work, barely able to find the strength to feed herself or her little corgis, and there were many a night where she came home in tears, crying herself to sleep wondering what she had done to deserve this treatment from so many people.

There were times she felt as if she just could not go on any longer and wondered how this would all end, almost hoping that it would be over soon. Her precious Ramsey and Skomer were there to greet her at the door every night, and the mistress would stoop down to both of the little dogs, burying her head in their fur, crying and crying until she just could not cry any more. Their hair would be soaked from their beloved mistress' tears and it broke their hearts to see what was once a happy, healthy person dissolve into such sadness and frailty, right before their eyes. Ramsey and Skomer would come and sit with her on the couch, cuddling on her lap or snuggling next to her for hours on end in the evenings while she slowly but surely regained her strength and resolve, with the help and support of family and friends and the good doctor. Whenever their mistress felt like giving up, Ramsey and Skomer would jump up next to her and nudge her as if to say, keep going, keep going...everything will be all right. She knew that she must not give up faith and the tiny, pale mistress believed with all her heart that the truth would prevail sooner or later. She just hoped that it would be sooner rather than later.

Her money and health were running out and their mistress worried what she would do if she could not keep their little house in the woods, and how her precious corgis would survive without her, not to mention all the little creatures in her yard that depended on her for food and sustenance. Bills were mounting up and her leave time at work was dwindling down, and the stress of it all was placing a further burden on the little mistress' health. Then one day, another break came for them all as a man at work stood up for her, and then another, and then another, until the truth came tumbling out like water over a dam that wild horses could not hold back now.

Each day as their mistress grew stronger in body, heart and spirit, she would come home to her faithful corgis, and their undying love spurred her on and gave her the will to live and persevere. Without them, there would have been no one in the little cottage at night to comfort her, and in those dark and lonely hours, sickness can come and steal a body away to those places where one does not wish to go until there is no more hope in this lifetime. The little corgis were always there to give her a smile and a kiss and their mistress would watch their playful antics, and it helped her to remember and embrace what a joyful life it had been and could be again in time, when the body had a chance to heal. The corgis knew that their mistress would make it back to health because after all, she had ancestors who came from the United Kingdom and the "Irish" in her literally willed her back to vigor, along with many prayers to God to bring their little family back together again as in days gone by, with happiness of heart, good health and most importantly, the love and devotion of the two best little corgis a person could ever have! Yes, it was a wonderful life again, indeed!

Chapter Twenty

One More Surprise

There was still one more surprise in store for Ramsey and Skomer. Just when they thought life could not get any better, there was a turn and twist in the road that brought much happiness to them all!

For years, the dogs lived with their mistress, just the three of them, in the little cottage in the woods and were as happy as any person and two dogs had a right to be, almost. Something was missing as their mistress would see couples holding hands or stealing a kiss or quick embrace and she would longingly wish that she had a special someone to love too, other than her precious corgis. Of course, corgis generally speaking feel that they are enough for anyone, and why would anybody want another person in their life when they had them? Corgis can be a bit self-centered, you know, but we can easily forgive them this one tiny fault, since they are pretty near perfect in every other respect.

Ramsey and Skomer were none too fond of several of her male companions who came to take their mistress out to dinner as they really did not like sharing her company with anyone, and on occasion, the corgis were known to put a man in his place and let him discover who really were the bosses in that house, just in case any of them had ideas about taking their mistress away from them. In fact, Ramsey and Skomer were notorious for taking an occasional little nip at the heels of a male visitor, or intruders as they cared to refer to their mistress' dates, just to put the fear of God in those who might be a bit shaky or squeamish. It was one way to sort out the men from the boys, so to speak.

One fine day, a man came to visit their mistress, and before Ramsey and Skomer even knew what was happening, the gentleman upon entry into the little cottage, got down on the floor and hugged and kissed the corgis, talking ever so sweetly to them both, that they didn't even have time to get their "bad act" together. It had been so long since Ramsey had felt the gentleness of a man's kind, but firm, touch that he had almost forgotten how special it was when his beloved master in Wales had reached down each evening to pet him after a good days work in the fields, and there was just nothing like it ever that could begin to compare to that special touch. Skomer, upon looking over at Ramsey, decided to follow his lead since he was the alpha dog after all, and suddenly she stopped her shaking and cowering (as she still suffered flashbacks from her mistreatment at the hand of someone long ago). Instinctively she licked the gentleman's hands over and over again, forgetting that she normally would follow the "bad act" routine also to frighten off any suitors.

The mistress looked on in amazement, hardly believing what her eyes were seeing and at that moment, she knew that this man was the one for her, because anyone who could love a dog like that would surely love her tenfold! The mistress and the kind gentleman began to spend more and more time together, laughing and talking about the future and what life has to bring, and the four of them whiled away many an evening hour, cuddled up on the sofa, with the corgis right there in between them. They were all snug as a bug in a rug.

Christmas Eve was upon them and after dinner and church, the gentleman was sitting on the sofa next to the three of them, as usual, when he pulled out a brown paper bag from his coat pocket and took out a little black velvet box, handing it to their mistress. The corgis were all excited because, you know, corgis like presents too and they could not wait to see what was in this tiny box. Their mistress sat motionless, almost as if she was in shock, and finally the gentleman asked her if she was going to just sit there or was she going to open her present. At that moment, she uncovered the gift and a sparkling treasure gleamed in the lamplight, and the gentleman asked for her hand (and their corgi paws) in marriage! Their mistress was overcome with emotion, and for the first time in her life was totally speechless. The gentleman repeated the question several more times, and the mistress finally came out of her stupor and said that she would be delighted and honored to be his wife! The corgis hopped off the sofa and danced around and frolicked with glee, wagging their little corgi behinds, hardly believing that they now were going to have a master too! They were all going to be one big happy family and they could barely contain themselves.

85

It had been many years with just the three of them, but they would gladly accept this new person into their lives as they saw how much joy and happiness he brought to their beloved mistress. He loved dogs, so what else could a corgi possibly ask for?

December really was Ramsey and Skomer's month as they found their "forever home" in a December and now found their "forever dad" in another December, too!

The days and weeks before and after the wedding with all the plans and merry chaos were some of the happiest times of the little corgis lives. Of course, the corgis attended the wedding, albeit uninvited.

The happy couple decided to get married in the little cottage in the woods, with only family and close friends attending the ceremony. The corgis were supposed to wait patiently in the bedroom until after the wedding was over and all the guests had departed. Corgis love people, music and food, so as you can see, a wedding was a winning triple combination! The corgis listened intently in the bedroom as the guests began to arrive and they could smell a delicious dinner cooking in the kitchen for all the guests to enjoy after the ceremony. They heard the joyous laughter of the guests arriving and it slowly but surely became just too much for the little corgis to handle. After all, they were close family too and felt they had every right to witness the wedding and take in all the merriment and excitement of this event first hand! The music began and all the guests were seated. Just as the minister asked, "Who gives this hand in marriage?" the corgis burst out of the bedroom and ran down the hallway into the living room where the ceremony was taking place, barking and barking with joy and excitement! Everyone turned and looked at the little dogs, laughing. At that, the minister replied, "Well, I guess that means the corgis do!" The mistress' father replied, " I couldn't have said it better myself." They now had everything that they had ever wished for – a warm, loving home with a new family that cared for each other and especially for two little rescue corgis that no one had wanted.

As the years went by and their mistress and master grew a little grayer, and the corgis had more corgi aches and pains from their days of neglect before they found their "forever home," they all were provided for, and the corgis were especially well taken care of in their latter years by the smartest and most wonderful lady veterinarian there ever was, who loved them as if they were her own.

Ramsey suffered severe arthritis of the spine from those horrible years in the outdoor pen and needed daily medications to alleviate his pain. All the family looked after him, with his Grammy and Grampy assisting with his care when his "forever mom and dad" were away at work. It was a labor of love for everyone, as they would never forget how Ramsey had brought such joy and happiness to their lives, saving his mistress from such sadness and misery during her darkest hours. It was the least they could do for Ramsey, and even that would never begin to repay their debt to him.

Little Skoie was also loved like there was no tomorrow, and it was easy to overlook her idiosyncrasies from years of abuse prior to her finding her way back to Ramsey and her "forever mom." One always knew where to look for Skoie, as she would be sitting right in her mother's lap or in her mother's arms, being a little bundle of energy and love. She was the apple of her mother's eye and gave so much joy to everyone who knew her, and all she asked in return was that you love her.

Throughout the years, there were many kind people

who helped these rescue dogs along the way – from the rescue lady and rescue organization, to local veterinarians who were their guardian angels, to their foster mother who prepared them for their "forever home," to a wonderful vet assistant who "baby-sat" the corgis when their master was away, to their adoring Grammy and Grampy who helped take care of them in sickness in their elder years, and last, but certainly not least, their dear master and mistress whose lives and hearts belonged to these corgis. All loved these magnificent dogs, but never to the depth or extent of the love that Ramsey and Skomer gave back to all who rescued them from a life that is still too sad to want to remember. Instead, theirs was a life of love, devotion, and happiness for years and years to come.

Courage comes in many forms, but none is as great as the undying duty of a dog to save his master nor that of a master to save his faithful dog and loyal friend.

Chapter Twenty-One

Epilogue

There is an old Scottish poem that sums up the tale of these courageous corgis and it goes like this.

> The one who listens when I talk,
> The one who cheers my lonely walk,
> The one who nuzzles when I cry,
> The one who comforts when I sigh,
>
> Who else could match my every mood?
> Who else would feast on scraps of food?
> Who else would prompt this monologue?
> Who else but you...
> My loving dog.

The courageous little corgis will never be forgotten. And they all lived happily ever after.

THE END

Bibliography

"Bless the Beasts and the Children...," quote from song by same title. Words and music by Barry DeVorzon and Perry Botkin, Jr.

"Give Me Your Tired Your Poor...," quote from poem "The New Colossus," by Emma Lazarus.

"My Dog," Scottish Poem. Author Unknown.